Raghupati Raghav Raja Ram

Patit Paavan Sita Ram

Ishwar Allah Tero Naam

Sabko Sanmati De Bhagwan

Lord of the Raghu dynasty – King Rama

Benefactor of the weak – Sita's Rama

God and Allah are your names – O Rama

Bless us all with wisdom – Lord Rama

Based on a hymn by the seventeenth-century
Marathi saint Ramdas.
This version composed by Vishnu Digambar Paluskar
was one of Mahatma Gandhi's favourite songs.

Anma, Tell Me About Ramayana!

Written by
Bhakti Mathur

Illustrated by
Maulshree Somani

Klaka excitedly hopped on to Amma's lap
As soon as it was time for their story today,
Amma had promised him the story of Rama!
And he had been waiting for it all day.

Amma started, "Ramayana is an ancient poem
Written by the great poet, Valmiki,
About the life and deeds of Prince Rama.
Listen closely, dear Klaka and Kiki.

Once upon a time, in a land called Ayodhya,
Ruled a mighty king whose name was Dasratha.
Blessed he was with four brave sons, called
Rama, Lakshmana, Bharat and Shatrughana.

Prince Rama, the oldest, was loved by all -
His virtues knew no bounds.
Kind, wise and brave, a warrior
Unmatched on the battleground.

When the time came for the new king to be named,
Dasratha chose Rama, who else could it be?
All of Ayodhya was thrilled with joy
And celebrated the news with glee.

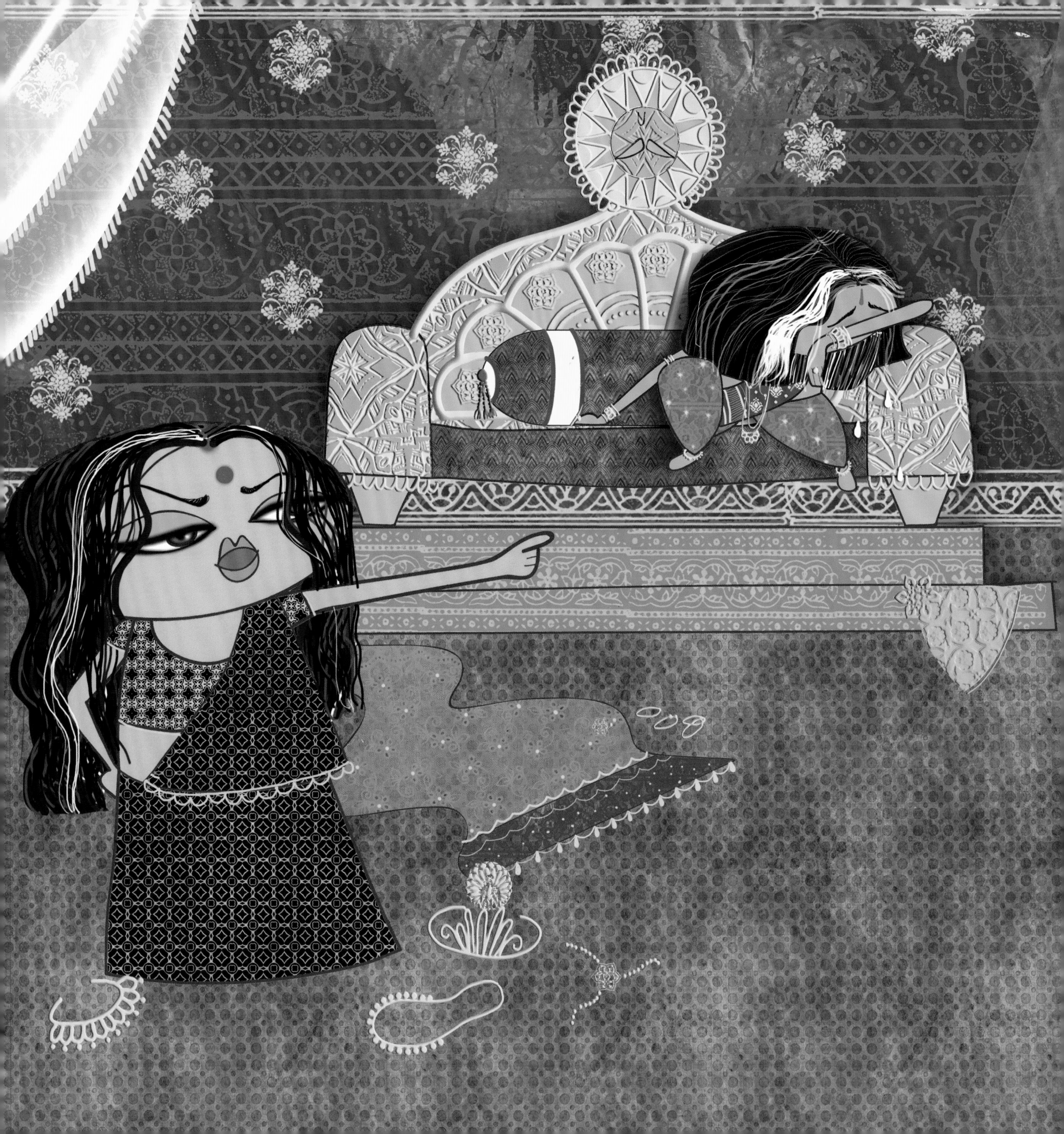

All except Kaikeyi, Rama's wicked step mother,
Who wanted Bharat, her son, as king of the land.
Mad with anger, she threw a big tantrum
And forced Dasratha to listen to her demands.

She said to Dasratha, "I saved you many years ago,
As wounded in battle you lay, tired and weak.
In return, you promised me two boons;
That you would provide whatever I seek.

My son, Bharat, must be the new king.
This is the first boon; fulfill it.
The second: banish Rama for fourteen years
To the forest to live as a hermit."

On hearing this, the king was shocked!
His heart was torn in two.
He was duty bound to keep every promise,
But exiling Rama, he couldn't bear to do.

But Rama was calm and consoled the king.
"Father, my duty is clear," said he.
"Happily I give up the throne and leave,
To keep your word to Queen Kaikeyi."

His wife, Sita, and his brother Lakshmana,
Said "Rama, we will come too.
Our place is by your side,
We cannot live without you."

And so, dressed only as simple hermits,
The three left the royal palace behind.
Bravely they strode to the forest ahead,
With dharma foremost on their minds.

The people of Ayodhya bade them farewell,
With tears streaming down their faces.
How would the three, who belonged to the palace,
Survive Dandaka forest - the darkest of places?

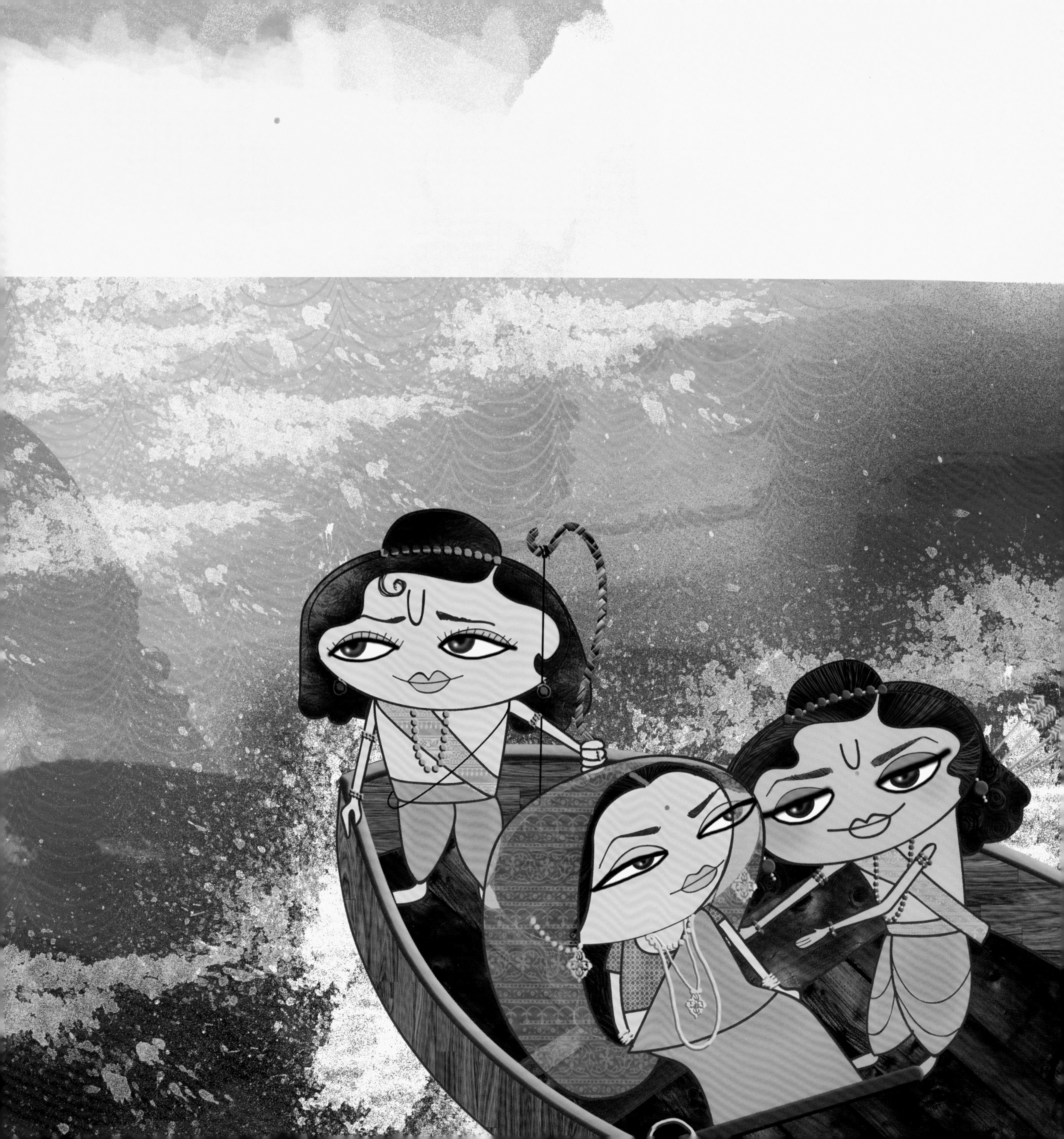

Dark and dangerous Dandaka forest was -
Full of wild animals and demons,
Terrorising people who lived nearby,
Causing havoc and killing innocent humans.

But Rama and Lakshmana were not afraid.
They fought the demons with a brave heart,
Cleared the forest of all that was evil,
And the gloom lifted and the darkness did part.

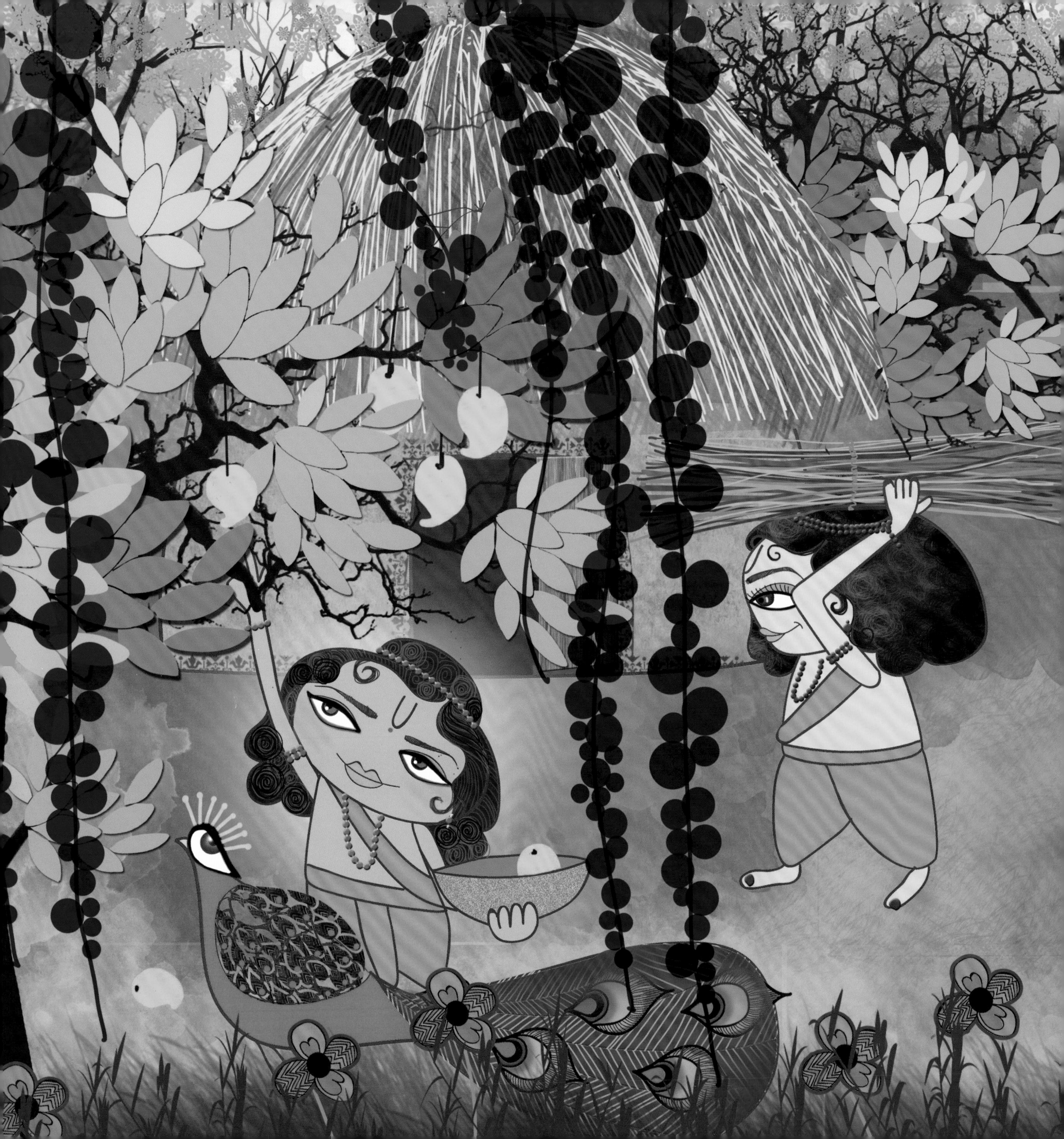

They soon got used to the simple life
In the forest they had made their own.
Working hard day and night, but happy
Very soon, thirteen years had flown.

But trouble lay in store ahead,
For Ravana, the ten-headed demon king,
Having heard of Sita's beauty,
Desired to make her his queen.

One day when Rama and Lakshmana were away,
Ravana came disguised as a beggar.
He pretended to ask Sita for food,
And tricked her out of her shelter.

He threw Sita into Pushpak, his chariot,
And swiftly it flew away
Across the ocean to Lanka, his kingdom,
Where he and his demons held sway.

When Rama and Lakshmana found Sita gone,
They were worried beyond belief.
Quickly they set off in search of her;
Rama could hardly control his grief.

Soon they came upon Jatayu,
The majestic lord of the birds.
But there he lay with his wing cut off,
Battered, in a pool of blood.

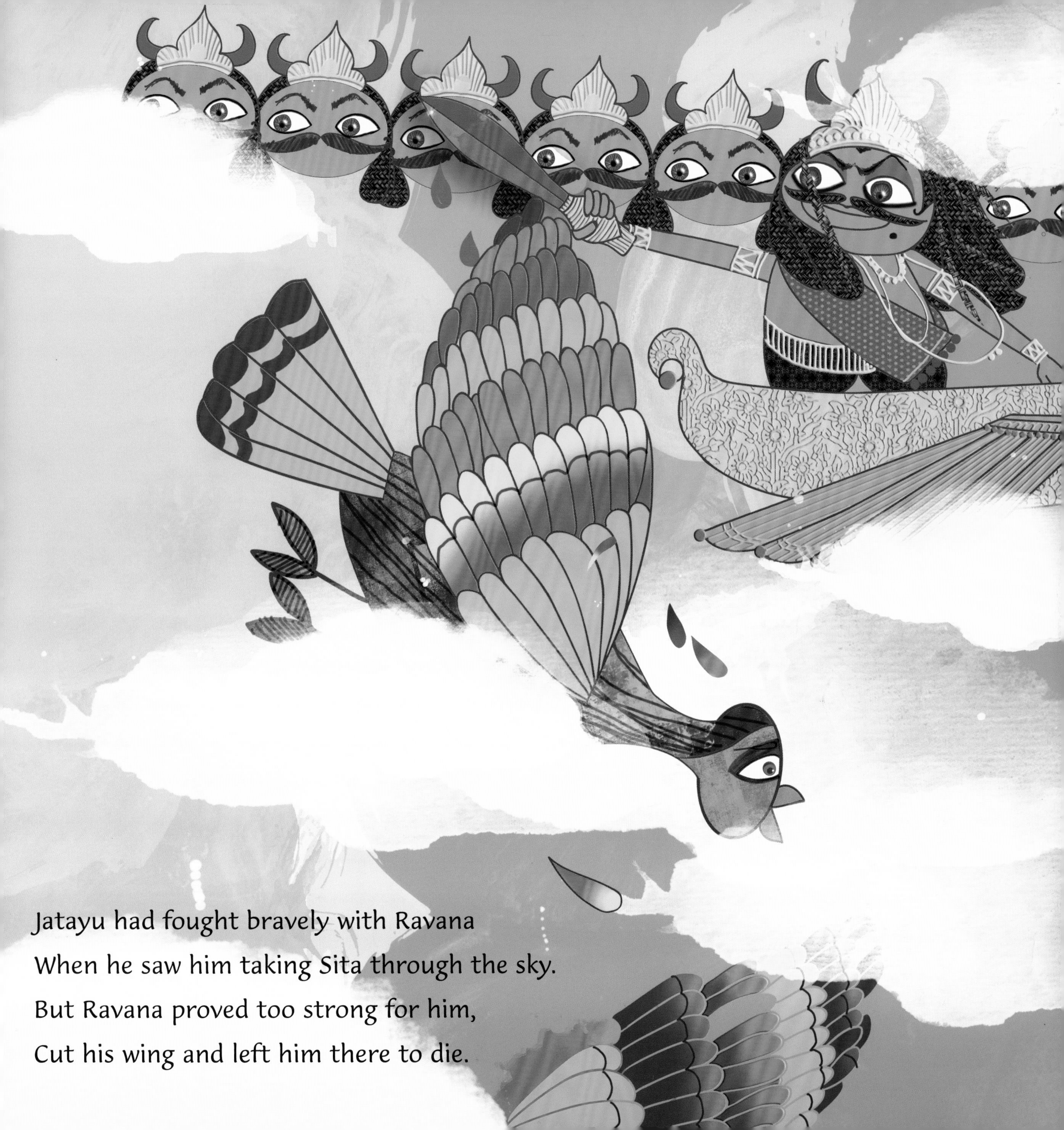

Jatayu had fought bravely with Ravana
When he saw him taking Sita through the sky.
But Ravana proved too strong for him,
Cut his wing and left him there to die.

"Ravana has Sita," Jatayu said.
"To Lanka he has taken her, and prevailed.
I tried my best to stop him,
But I am sorry, O Rama, that I failed."

"I can never thank you enough, O brave Jatayu,"
Replied Rama. "You've done so much for me.
The bravest and mightiest of birds are you.
Your name will go down in history."

Rama and Lakshmana set off at once
Towards Ravana and his Lanka.
On the way there they met Hanuman,
The general of the monkey kingdom, Kishkindha.

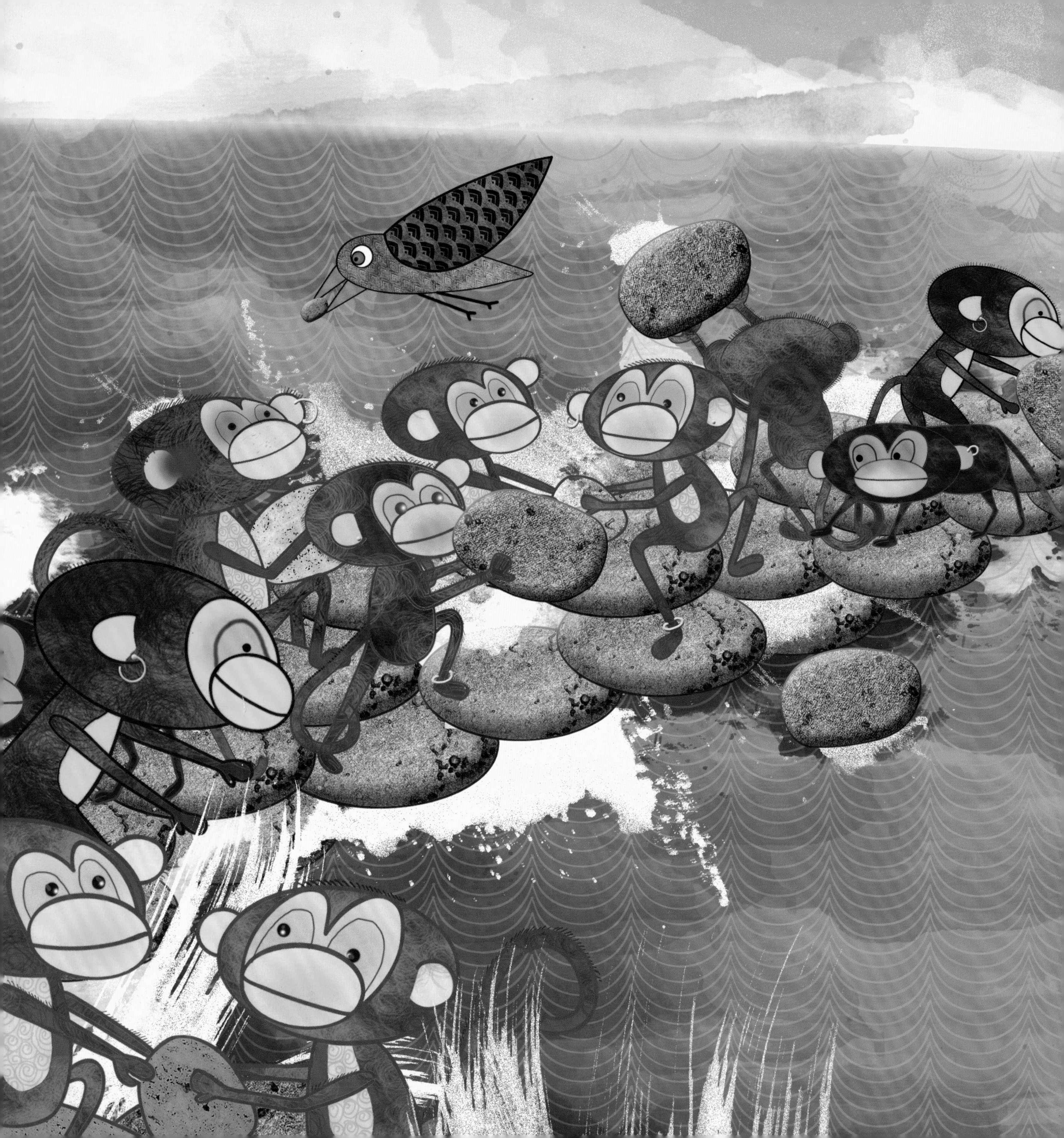

On hearing Rama's sorrowful tale,
Hanuman pledged his help, and with his aid,
Rama raised an army of monkeys and bears,
And marched towards Lanka, unafraid.

They finally reached the ocean,
And there was Lanka for all to see.
But this seemed the end of the road for them,
For how could they cross the mighty sea?

They sat for days at the ocean's edge;
Their efforts seemed a complete loss.
Finally, Rama prayed to the Sea God,
To help them find a way across.

The Sea God answered their prayers.
A miracle occurred as they watched in awe:
Stones and rocks started to float on water
And they built a bridge to reach Lanka's shore!

Then the war began
And it was a fearsome war!
People say that such a great war
Had never been fought before.

The monkey warriors were quick and strong;
They fought with courage and skill.
By Rama and Lakshmana's magical arrows,
Thousands of demons were killed.

But Ravana's demons also fought with valour,
And never did they seem to tire.
They fell upon the monkey army
And fought fire with fire.

Finally Rama and Ravana met,
And a fearsome duel did ensue.
Rama's arrow cut off Ravana's head,
But in its place, a new one grew.

Ten times did Rama
Cut off Ravana's head,
And ten times a new one
Sprang up in its stead!

Then Rama remembered that Ravana's navel
Was the place where his life force did flow.
Taking a flaming golden arrow,
Rama released it from his bow.

As the arrow hit Ravana's navel,
Time seemed to stand still.
Very slowly he fell to the ground -
The evil demon was finally killed.

Then Sita came out of Lanka,
Her gentle face shining with love and life.
Rama could not wait anymore
And ran towards his beloved wife.

As Rama and Sita embraced each other,
The clouds in the sky parted ways.
The entire earth lit up with joy,
With the brightness of the sun's rays.

The fourteen years of Rama's exile
Had finally come to an end.
It was time to return to Ayodhya,
Their beloved home once again.

With the three on his back, mighty Hanuman
Flew to Ayodhya that very night.
As they got nearer the city,
They were guided by thousands of lights!

You see, the people of Ayodhya,
For fourteen years, had counted each day.
They lit diyas all across the city
To show their beloved Rama the way.

Rama was crowned king of Ayodhya;
It was a joyous celebration.
For many years his rule did last.
He reigned over a happy, just nation.

So that was the story of Rama, dear Klaka and Kiki,
An epic tale that has lots to teach you.
How you too can be like Rama,
Learn his goodness and embody his virtue.

Learn from Lakshmana, the loyal brother,
And from Sita, the perfect woman and wife.
Learn from Hanuman how true love for Rama
Can guide you through your life!"

Glossary

Amma: Mother

Ayodhya: An ancient city in India and the birthplace of Rama. The city is named after King Ayudh, the founder of the city and one of the forefathers of Rama. The name Ayodhya means 'unconquerable'.

Dasratha: Rama's father and a king of Ayodhya. The word Dasratha means 'one who can drive ten chariots at the same time.'

Dharma: A concept of central importance in Indian philosophy and religion, it means that which upholds or supports the natural order of things. It refers to one's personal obligations, calling and duties.

Diya(s): An oil lamp usually made from clay, with a cotton wick dipped in ghee or vegetable oils.

Hanuman: A general among the vanars, an ape-like race of forest dwellers. He has the ability to expand to the size of a mountain or shrink down to the size of a mouse. He is strong and clever, and a loyal and faithful friend.

Jatayu: A demigod who has the form of a vulture. He was an old friend of Dasratha.

Kaikeyi: The second of King Dasratha's three wives and a queen of Ayodhya. She was the mother of Bharat.

Lakshmana: Rama's brother and close companion. He is known for his loyalty and his love for Rama.

Rama: The seventh avatar or incarnation of Lord Vishnu, who came to Earth to destroy Ravana, the demon king.

Ravana: The ruler of Lanka and the king of the demon race called the rakshasas. Ravana achieved the utmost degree of wickedness and was the very incarnation of evil. He is said to have possessed the nectar of immortality, which was stored under his navel, thanks to a celestial boon by Brahma.

Sita: Rama's wife. Her name is derived from a Sanskrit word which means furrow, as her father, King Janaka, found her in a furrow in a ploughed field. She is also regarded as an incarnation of Goddess Lakshmi, the wife of Lord Vishnu.

Valmiki: Author of the epic Ramayana. Revered as the 'Adi Kavi' or 'First Poet', for he discovered the first verse which defined the form of Sanskrit poetry. Valmiki was a highway robber in his early life. To atone for his sins, he meditated on Rama for so long that an anthill grew around him and hence he got the name Valmiki, which means anthill in Sanskrit.